· LITTLE HOUSE ·

Rose #5

Missouri School Days

ADAPTED FROM THE ROSE YEARS BOOKS BY
Roger Lea MacBride

ILLUSTRATED BY
Doris Ettlinger

HarperTrophy®
A Division of HarperCollinsPublishers

Adaptation by Heather Henson.

HarperCollins®, ☎®, Little House®, Harper Trophy®, and The Rose Years™
are trademarks of HarperCollins Publishers Inc.

Missouri School Days
Text adapted from *Little Farm in the Ozarks*, text copyright 1994
by Roger Lea MacBride; *In the Land of the Big Red Apple*,
text copyright 1995 by Roger Lea MacBride; *On the Other Side of the Hill*,
text copyright 1995 by the Estate of Roger Lea MacBride.
Illustrations by Doris Ettlinger
Illustrations copyright © 2001 by Renée Graef

Library of Congress Cataloging-in-Publication Data
MacBride, Roger Lea, 1929–
  Missouri school days / adapted from the Rose years books by Roger Lea
MacBride ; illustrated by Doris Ettlinger.—1st ed.
    p.   cm.—(A little house chapter book)
  "The Rose chapter book collection."
  Summary: After moving from South Dakota, Rose Wilder eventually makes
friends, proves herself to be the best speller in her class, and copes with a
difficult teacher at her new Missouri school.
  ISBN 0-06-028555-9 (lib. bdg.) — ISBN 0-06-442110-4 (pbk.)
  1. Lane, Rose Wilder, 1886–1968—Juvenile fiction. [1. Lane, Rose Wilder,
1886–1968—Fiction.   2. Wilder, Laura Ingalls, 1867–1957—Family—Fiction.
3. Frontier and pioneer life—Missouri—Fiction.   4. Schools—Fiction.
5. Missouri—Fiction.]   I. Ettlinger, Doris, ill.   II. Title.   III. Series.
PZ7.M926 Mk   2001   00-38833
[Fic]—dc21

Typography by Carla Weise
1 2 3 4 5 6 7 8 9 10
❖
First Harper Trophy Edition, 2001

Contents

CHAPTER 1

New Girl

Rose waded across the creek. She held up the hem of her dress carefully so it wouldn't get wet. The cool water felt good on her bare feet. But it couldn't wash away her jitters. Today was the first day of school.

Back in South Dakota, Rose had loved school. But now she lived in the Ozark Mountains of Missouri, in a little house on an apple farm. Mama and Papa had brought her here in a wagon the year before. Rose liked Missouri, but she didn't think she would like being the new girl in school.

Slowly Rose trudged up the long hill that stood between home and school. It was summer and the sun was already high. The air was warm. Yellow daisies were everywhere.

When she reached the top of the hill, Rose stopped. She could see the tall brick schoolhouse below. She could see swarms of children walking along the road. Boys were playing on the playground.

Rose looked for her friends Paul and George Cooley, but she could not find them. The Cooleys had made the long journey from South Dakota to Missouri with Rose's family. Rose loved to play with Paul and George, but she did not see them very often. They lived in town and helped their folks run a hotel.

Rose took a deep breath and started down the slope. Her heart pounded in her chest. When she reached the bottom of the hill, she heard the bell ring. All the children raced toward the big front door. Rose hurried not to be last. Everyone pushed and jostled and laughed.

Finally Rose was inside. A tall man with a long beard was telling everyone where to go. He looked right at Rose.

"You there, little girl in the plaid," he shouted. "What reader are you in?"

Rose did not know what to say, but the man saw the book Mama had given her.

"Third Reader, to the right," he said, pointing the way.

Rose walked through another door into a classroom. A boy rushed past her, knocking her dinner pail to the floor. She picked it up and looked around. Rows and rows of double desks lined the room. The floor was shiny bright yellow wood.

There were many great tall windows all around the three walls and a large heating stove against one wall. The opposite wall from the stove was partly painted black. That was the blackboard.

Children were racing about the room, shouting and arguing over seats. Rose did not know where to sit.

Suddenly the man with the beard was talking to her again.

"Have a seat, please. Put your dinner pail on the shelf and sit anywhere on the girls' side."

Rose put up her dinner pail and looked around the room. Every seat seemed to be taken. Then she spotted an empty one at the front, next to a girl with beautiful curly black hair falling in ringlets. She wore a lovely dress and shiny black shoes. Rose liked to sit in front, so she went to sit in that desk.

But when she put down her book on the desktop, the girl turned and frowned at her.

"You can't sit here," she said. "It's my friend's seat. She's coming in a minute."

Rose flushed hot. She stood in front

of all those desks of strangers, not knowing what to do or where to go. Several children were staring at her. Two girls sitting together whispered to each other and pointed at her.

Finally Rose saw an empty seat in the back row. She almost ran down the aisle and quickly sat in it. She was happy to be where no one could stare at her.

Rose looked at her seatmate. Her head was resting on her hands on the desk, her face turned away from Rose.

"Hello," Rose said politely. "My name is Rose Wilder."

The girl looked at Rose blankly.

"I'm tired," she said. Then she wiped her nose with the back of her hand and laid her head down again.

Rose's heart began to sink. There was no sign of Paul or George. They were older, so they would be upstairs in the Fourth Reader.

Just then the man with the beard brought them all to attention.

"My name is Professor Kay," he announced. He wrote his name on the blackboard in chalk. Then he took the roll. He called out many names.

"Blanche Coday," he called, and the girl with the beautiful black hair answered, "Present, sir."

Rose remembered seeing Coday's Drugs on a trip to town with Papa. She noticed that Blanche's seatmate was very pretty, too. Her blond hair hung in a silky braid down her back. Her white dress had a butterfly pattern on it.

Finally all the names on the roll were called, including Irene Strong, the girl sitting next to Rose. Every name had been called except Rose's.

"Is there any scholar here whose name I did not call?"

Rose raised her hand.

"Stand up, please," Professor Kay said. He pointed a long stick at her. Everyone in the room turned to look at Rose. Her neck blazed hot under all those eyes. "What is your name, please?"

"Rose Wilder," Rose whispered.

"Speak up; I can't hear you."

Titters rippled around the room.

Rose said her name again.

"Very well," the teacher said. "Please be seated."

Rose hated being stared at and laughed at. And the desk seat was too tall and the room was too hot. A trickle of sweat ran down Rose's back.

Rose had never had a teacher who was

a man. She had loved Miss Barrow, her teacher in South Dakota. Miss Barrow was pretty, and she had a beautiful voice. Back in South Dakota Rose had had many friends to play with.

Now Rose had only one thought: to run out of that school and all the way home. She would go home and she would never come back. But she did not budge from her seat. She was too shy to run away.

Then the lessons began. Professor Kay started with recitations. He called on the boys first.

Rose grew bored waiting her turn. She was the very last to go. Finally Teacher asked her to recite two paragraphs from a book she knew almost by heart. She recited easily.

"Very well done," Professor Kay said when she was finished.

Rose knew she should have been pleased, but she didn't care. She knew all of her Third Reader. She had even read the Fourth and Fifth Reader. She had read *The Adventures of Robinson Crusoe*, and she often read the newspaper Papa brought home. Mama had been a teacher before she married Papa, and she had taught Rose well.

So Rose sat there, prickly hot. Finally Professor Kay rang a tiny bell that he kept on his desk. That meant it was time for recess.

Rose could hardly wait to see Paul and George. She raced outside with all the other children and waited by the front door. Paul came clomping noisily down the stairs with two other boys. His face lit up when he saw Rose.

"Hey, Rose!" he said.

 10

Just then another boy called out. All the boys raced around to one side of the schoolhouse to play a game.

"See you later!" Paul shouted. Then he dashed off to follow them.

George came racing out of the schoolhouse. He shouted hello to Rose and ran off to play, too.

So Rose was by herself. She saw Blanche Coday and a group of town girls in pretty dresses playing house with some rocks. But they did not invite Rose to join them, and she was too shy to ask.

Some other children were playing crack-the-whip, but Rose did not feel like joining in. She looked longingly at the hill she had walked down that morning. She missed Mama and Papa and her little dog, Fido. She didn't think she would ever like going to school in Missouri.

CHAPTER 2

Afternoon Lessons

At noon, Rose was alone again. Paul and George went back to the hotel to eat dinner with their mama and papa. The other children who stayed at school sat in groups with friends or brothers and sisters. Rose sat by herself under a tree at the edge of the playground.

In her dinner pail, she found two pieces of brown bread with bacon fat spread on them, a boiled potato, and a dried-apple turnover.

Twin girls sat near her. They were dressed exactly the same, in sprigged green calico. Their hair was fixed exactly the same, in tidy buns on the tops of their heads. Out of their large pail they each took a piece of fried chicken and a biscuit.

"You're a new girl, aren't you?" one of the twins said. "Come and eat with us. We like to meet new girls."

"Thank you," Rose said gratefully. She picked up her things and sat down next to the twins.

"My name is Dora," one of the girls said. "This is my sister, Cora. We're the Hibbard twins. What's your name?"

"Rose Wilder," said Rose.

"You aren't in the Fourth Reader," said Dora.

"I'm in the Third Reader," Rose told her. "This is my first day in school. I used

to live in South Dakota."

"I know where that is," Cora said proudly.

Rose liked chatting with the twins. Dora and Cora were like one person, split in half. Even their voices were exactly the same. Rose wondered how anyone could tell them apart.

After they had finished their dinner, Dora and Cora and Rose joined a group of girls who were playing cat and mouse. Rose liked cat and mouse. It felt so good to be running and laughing and giggling along with everyone else.

When the bell rang, Rose said good-bye to Dora and Cora. As she went back to her seat, she thought about how lucky twins were. They always had a best friend to play with.

After recess was spelling. Professor Kay drew a long, straight chalk mark on the floor at the front of the classroom. Everyone stood on it in a line, in alphabetical order, facing Professor Kay. Rose's name was last so she stood at the foot of the line.

Teacher called out a word and each student took a turn spelling. Spelling was Rose's best subject, and she knew all the words.

She repeated each word Professor Kay

gave her and then spelled it. Every time she correctly spelled a word that some-one else had misspelled, she got to move up one place in line. Rose felt a tingle of excitement each time she got a word right. Soon she had spelled down two students, and she was third from the end.

All afternoon they spelled. Rose moved up the line, closer and closer to the head. She was getting closer to Blanche Coday. Blanche had spelled down the two boys who were ahead of her.

Finally Rose stood next to Blanche. She was only one word away from being the best speller in the class that day. Her stomach quivered, her hands were cold, and her palms were damp. She wanted more than anything to spell down Blanche Coday.

But Blanche was a good speller, too.

 16

Every word Professor Kay gave her she spelled correctly. Every time she got one right, Blanche looked at Rose smugly. But every word Professor Kay gave Rose, Rose spelled correctly, too.

The next time it was Blanche's turn, Professor Kay said, *"Chiefly."*

Rose knew that word, too. She crossed her fingers behind her back.

"Chiefly," Blanche said, tossing her head so her curls shook. "C-h-e-i-f-l-y."

Rose trembled with joy. She knew Blanche had made a mistake. She knew the rule by heart: "*i* before *e*, except after *c*." Blanche had gotten it wrong! Rose could hardly stand still.

"Wrong," said Professor Kay. "Next."

Blanche shot a hard, pinched look at Rose.

"Chiefly," Rose said with confidence.

"C-h-i-e-f-l-y."

"Very good," said Professor Kay. He wrote Rose's name on a corner of the blackboard and put a mark next to it. That was a head mark. It meant that Rose had gotten to the head of the line by spelling down all the other scholars.

"That will be all for today. Class is dismissed," Professor Kay announced.

Everyone scrambled to leave. Rose picked up her book, her slate, and her dinner pail and bounded out of school. She ran all the way home. Fido rushed up the wagon track to meet her, barking with joy.

Rose was never so glad to be home. But she felt good about the spelling bee. Girls like Blanche might laugh at her, but she could beat any of them in spelling.

 18

CHAPTER 3

Spelldown

Slowly the weeks passed, and Rose did not mind school so much. She often sat with Dora and Cora at recess and dinner. They talked or played cat and mouse with the other girls.

Every day when the bell rang for afternoon lessons, there was spelling. Every day Rose started at the foot and ended at the head. She always spelled down Blanche Coday. But even though they ended up standing next to each other,

19

Blanche did not speak to Rose, and Rose was too shy to speak to Blanche.

Finally September came, and the last day of the summer school session drew near. Professor Kay announced that there would be a special spelldown on Friday after supper. Each class would have its own spelldown. All the mothers and fathers were invited to come. There would be refreshments and a prize for the winner. Then there would be no more school until after harvest time.

Rose was excited and jittery all that week. Every time she thought about the spelldown, her insides quivered. She knew she could win. She had gotten almost all the head marks in the class. But Blanche was getting better and better. She had gotten three head marks when Rose made mistakes. All that week, Rose stole anxious glances at Blanche studying her reader.

Finally Friday arrived. After supper Rose washed up and changed into her best calico. Mama had washed and ironed it. Together Rose, Mama, and Papa walked to school. The schoolyard was teeming with wagons and horses. People were streaming in from every direction, dressed up and in a festive, friendly mood.

Inside the classroom, Rose saw Blanche standing with her parents. Blanche's best dress was even more beautiful than the dresses she wore every day. It was made from a soft red material and was trimmed with satin that shimmered in the light.

Professor Kay said it was time for the spelldown to begin. He asked all the parents to be seated. Then he had all the students stand in line as usual. Rose liked her place at the foot of the line. It made her less nervous to hear other students making mistakes.

Each time Rose spelled a word correctly, Papa winked at her and Mama smiled.

One by one the students were spelled down and left the line to join their families. At last Rose and Blanche were the only ones left standing. Rose felt every eye in the room on her.

Blanche spelled every word correctly, but so did Rose. On and on they spelled into the evening. Rose's mouth was dry, and her legs ached a little. She longed to sit down.

Then Professor Kay gave Blanche the word *precipice*.

Blanche said the word slowly, and then she spelled, "p-r-e-c-i-p-i-s-e."

"Oh!" someone in the audience cried out. Papa slapped his hand on the desktop. Mama turned and shushed him.

At first Rose did not understand what had happened. Then Professor Kay said, "Wrong."

Rose could hardly believe her ears. She knew how to spell that word. Blanche had got it wrong!

Professor Kay looked at Rose and repeated the word.

"*Precipice,*" said Rose. "P-r-e-c-i-p-i-c-e."

The room erupted in a swirl of shouting and clapping. Suddenly all the people were on their feet, moving about and talking. Professor Kay was saying something about lemonade on the second floor. Then Mama and Papa came pushing through the crowd up to Rose. Papa gave her a big hug. Mama smiled her biggest smile.

Rose realized with a shock that she had actually won the spelldown.

"That's our smart girl," Papa said.

"We are very proud of you," said Mama.

Professor Kay congratulated Rose and gave her a prize. Rose took it in her hands. It was a book, thickly covered with plush. The plush was deep red, soft as moss. On the cover in shiny gold lettering was the word *Autographs*.

Inside the book all the pages were blank, with beautiful curlicue borders printed in pale blue. Mama said it was an album, for friends and loved ones to write little sayings or poems in. It was a place to keep memories of good friends and special times.

"Every girl must have one," said Mama. "I did."

"Thank you, Professor Kay," Rose said

politely. Inside she was jumping with joy. She looked around excitedly. Then she saw Blanche across the room. She was standing with her mother and father, and she was crying.

Rose looked at the beautiful new album, and then back at Blanche. She wondered what she could do. Blanche had not been nice to Rose, but Rose did not hate her, and she did not like to see anyone cry.

Suddenly Rose walked across the room, right up to Blanche's family.

"Why hello there, young lady," said Mr. Coday. "You really gave us quite a show here tonight."

Blanche turned to look at Rose. Her cheeks were damp and her face was blotched. Her mouth pinched into a frown.

"Please don't cry," said Rose. "I'm

sorry you lost. I almost lost first. I couldn't remember if *occasion* has one *c* or two. I only guessed. I was just lucky."

Blanche's frown softened. She looked down at the autograph album in Rose's hands.

"Professor Kay gave me this for winning. It isn't fair to give only one prize when we are such equally good spellers," said Rose. "We can share it if you like."

Rose held out the album and Blanche stared at it.

"Thank you," Blanche murmured. Then she smiled a little. "But it's your prize. You are very nice to offer."

Rose thought for a moment. Then she had another idea.

"Will you write in it, then?" Rose asked. "Since we are both the best spellers, I would like you to be the first

one to write in it."

"I . . . I wouldn't know what to write," Blanche stammered and blushed.

"Take it home with you," said Rose. "Then you can think of something."

"All right," said Blanche softly. She took the album from Rose, ran her hand over the mossy cover, and tucked it under her arm. She looked at Rose with shining eyes. "I'll take good care of it. I promise."

Since there would be no school till December, Blanche's father said he would give the album to Papa the next time he was in town.

"Good-bye, Blanche," Rose said.

"Good-bye, Rose," said Blanche.

Rose skipped back to be with Mama and Papa. She asked if they could go upstairs with everyone else to have lemonade.

"Very well," Mama laughed. "But where is your album?"

"I gave it to Blanche," said Rose. "She is going to write something in it."

"That's very sweet, Rose," said Mama. "Now I have two reasons to be proud of you tonight. A good winner is a gracious winner."

Blanche did not come upstairs to drink lemonade. Rose did not see her again that evening. But as she walked home by lantern light between Mama and Papa, Rose remembered Blanche's grateful smile. It made Rose happy to think she could make someone smile.

CHAPTER 4

Back to School

After Thanksgiving it was time for school to begin again. The first morning Rose was so jittery that her stomach hurt.

When Papa had brought her album back from Mr. Coday's store, Rose had tingled with excitement when she'd read what Blanche had written in pretty blue ink:

Too wise you are, too wise you be;
I see you are too wise for me.
Your friend, Blanche Coday.
October 3, 1895.

The words made Rose feel good. Blanche wanted to be her friend. But she also felt scared. How could she ever measure up to the way Blanche and the other town girls dressed? She still had only one school dress, and her old shoes were patched.

After breakfast Mama packed Rose's dinner. She tied Rose's blue ribbons around her braids and tied the sash of her pinafore. Then Rose put on her coat and headed out the door with her slate and pencil.

At Fry Creek Rose gave Fido a last scratch on the head, took off her shoes, and hitched her dress to wade across. The water was cold over her bare feet and ankles. They still ached when she reached the front door of the schoolhouse.

But Rose forgot all about her cold feet

31

as soon as she saw Blanche waiting in the hallway with a big smile on her face.

"Oh, hello, Rose!" Blanche cried out. "I was afraid you might not come."

"Hello, Blanche," Rose answered.

Blanche looped an arm through Rose's and tugged her into the classroom.

"Come quick!" she laughed. "Take off your coat and hang it next to mine. Put your dinner pail over here on the shelf. I saved seats for us at the front."

Rose's heart swelled with joy. As they walked through the classroom full of girls and boys, Rose felt none of the shyness of her first day.

Professor Kay, sitting at his desk in the front, greeted Rose heartily.

"Well, well, my star scholar returns. Hello, Miss Wilder."

Rose might not have pretty dresses

 32

and new shoes like the town girls, but she had a friend now, and everyone remembered that she had won the spelldown in September.

At noon Blanche walked home to eat her dinner. So Rose sat at her desk after she ate and read a book Professor Kay had lent her.

When Blanche came back, they sat together for afternoon lessons, whispering and passing notes they wrote on their slates.

"Harry Carnall is a terrible pest!" Blanche wrote. Harry was always bringing snakes and frogs and bugs to school to scare the girls.

"School is so DULL sometimes," wrote Rose.

The first Friday Rose made head in spelling, and Blanche was second. But they didn't quarrel, and Rose made sure to compliment Blanche for spelling an extra-hard word perfectly.

Blanche was so pretty and elegant. Rose loved to hear her stories about the goings-on in town.

"Yesterday there was an awful fight in front of the saloon," Blanche said one day. "The sheriff came and arrested both of the men."

Rose thought it must be wonderful to live in town where there were so many things to see and know about. She loved the farm, but sometimes she wondered what it would be like to be Blanche.

It felt cozy to have a friend at school, but Rose still felt shabby next to the town girls. They made her feel poor even thought Papa had said they weren't.

And Rose was bored with the lessons

35

in school. She was the best student. That meant she had to be still and listen to the other scholars reciting and learning lessons she knew already. Rose wanted to go on to Miss Pimberton's Fourth Reader classroom upstairs, with the older students. But Professor Kay said she was still too young.

So Rose was torn. She liked her new friend, but she still did not like school very much.

CHAPTER 5

Professor Crowe

The next year Rose finally moved up to the Fourth Reader. Blanche was moving up also. Dora and Cora and George Cooley would all be in that class, too.

This year Rose was looking forward to her first day of school for many reasons.

First of all, she had a new dress. It was a red calico sprigged with tiny yellow leaves and flowers. Rose had picked the cloth herself at Reynold's store with Mama. She also had a new hat Mama had made her of soft blue wool. The hat had a soft fuzzy ball on top. Mama called it a tam-o'-shanter. She said it was the kind of hat a Scot would wear.

Rose also had a donkey to ride to school so her feet wouldn't get cold crossing the creek. Papa had given her the donkey for her birthday. Rose had named it Spookendyke.

Finally Rose was happy because now she would have a new teacher. Rose had liked Professor Kay, but she liked lady teachers better. She knew that Miss Pimberton was young and pretty. And she'd heard that she was kind and pleasant, too.

When Rose got to school, she quickly hitched Spookendyke in the wooden shed with the other scholars' horses and mules and hurried inside. Rose knew right where to go. She dashed up the stairs to the second floor and burst into the Fourth Reader room.

Right away she spotted Blanche sitting in the front row, but she was sitting next to another girl!

Rose's heart sank. But then Blanche turned and saw her. Her face lit up with a big grin. She jumped up and ran between the desks.

"Oh, Rose," Blanche laughed. Her shiny black hair was curled. She was wearing a dress made of beautiful dark blue velvet with white satin collar, cuffs, and sash. "You must meet my cousin, Lydia. She's come from Chicago, and she's staying with us this winter. I saved a seat at the desk behind ours."

Rose felt glad again. Of course Blanche should sit with her cousin. Rose rushed to hang her new hat and coat in the girls'

cloakroom and put her dinner pail on the shelf.

Then she slid into the desk behind Blanche. She saw that she was sitting next to a girl wearing a brown and green gingham dress.

"Hello," Rose said. "My name is Rose Wilder."

"I'm Lula Faddis." The girl smiled.

Before Rose had time to chat with her seatmate, a man's deep voice bellowed from the back of the room.

"Silence in the Fourth Reader!"

Rose nearly jumped out of her seat. Instantly the room fell quiet. Everyone spun around to see who had shouted.

A tall man with a bushy black mustache and a bald head was scowling at them with fierce dark eyes. He held a long piece of cane in his hand.

Just then Harry Carnall snorted in the silence. The tall man strode between the rows of desks, straight to Harry. Without a word he grabbed Harry by the neck and lifted him off his seat.

"Ow! Ow! Ow!" Harry cried out as the man dragged him in front of the class.

"I am Professor Crowe," the man said in a thundering voice. Harry squirmed and sniffled, his face puckered with pain. But Professor Crowe would not let go. He laid the cane on his desk, picked up a piece of chalk, and wrote his name on the chalkboard. Harry wriggled in his other hand like a grasshopper stuck on a fishhook.

"I am your teacher and I will tolerate no foolishness!" he bellowed.

Rose scrunched down in her seat. She felt sorry for Harry. She wondered where

Miss Pimberton was. Her spirits began to sink.

At last Professor Crowe let poor Harry go. Harry stumbled to his seat, sniffling loudly.

"Take up your books!" Professor Crowe ordered.

Blanche turned to quickly look at Rose with big, frightened eyes. The old feeling Rose had of hating school came back in a rush. She felt even worse than before, because Professor Crowe was so mean.

All morning the boys and girls went through their recitations. Professor Crowe struck his desk hard with the cane switch when someone spoke out of turn or made a mistake. It made a terribly loud *crack!* that frightened Rose and made her skin burn hot.

Finally it was time for recess. All the

43

students grabbed their coats to go outside, even though the weather was cold. No one wanted to stay inside with Teacher.

"Oh, he's just awful!" Blanche wailed.

"What happened to Miss Pimberton?" Rose wondered.

"She got married and moved away," Blanche answered. She knew because her father was on the school committee.

"I wish I was back in Chicago," Lydia said mournfully.

After recess it was time for arithmetic. Professor Crowe stalked up and down the rows of desks, slapping his cane switch against his leg. In the middle of a problem, he stopped at Rose's desk. Rose was too frightened to look up from the figures she was writing on her slate.

"Where in the world did you learn to write like that?" he demanded.

Rose looked at her hand and arm. They were turned sideways to the slate. Ever since she was little in school in South Dakota, she had written that way. She'd sat on the left of a girl who was left-handed. There had been no room to write the way the other scholars did. So she learned to turn in her seat and write sideways.

"Well?" Professor Crowe's deep voice boomed out. "I am waiting for your answer."

Rose sat still as a statue, not knowing what to say. She could feel every eye in the room staring at her.

She managed to answer in a whisper, "It's the way I learned in my old school."

"You are not in your old school any longer," Professor Crowe quickly said. "You will write with your elbow at your side, sitting in the proper manner in your seat, or I shall have to tie your arm down until you learn."

Then he walked slowly down the row of desks, the switch slapping his leg.

Rose stared at her slate. She hated to be made fun of in front of the class. And she hated to be told what to do. Her spelling was perfect, and so was her penmanship. It didn't matter how she wrote. She could write hanging upside down in a tree if she wanted to.

The rest of that day was awful. In the afternoon Professor Crowe picked on George Cooley's spelling. Then he tied Elmer Stone's left hand to his leg with a rag to keep him from writing with it.

Poor Elmer struggled to write with his right hand, but his writing came out squiggly. Professor Crowe made him do his work over and over until Elmer nearly cried.

It was all Rose could do to stay inside that room. The only thing that kept her from jumping up and leaving were the sour looks she exchanged with the other children. They all hated Professor Crowe. And in hating him, they had all become friends.

CHAPTER 6

The Stove Prank

The next morning Rose awoke feeling a mix of dread and excitement. She didn't want to see Professor Crowe again. But she had heard some of the boys whispering that they would play a trick on him. She wanted to see if they would.

For the first time ever, Rose was early for school. When she came into class, two boys were carrying extra wood for the heating stove. After they piled the wood on the floor, Rose noticed them nudging the stove sideways a little with their feet.

48

They looked up at the long stovepipe that went into the ceiling and giggled. Rose didn't understand why.

Soon the room was filled with students. Then Professor Crowe arrived, clomping heavily up the stairs.

"Hurry, it's Teacher!" someone hissed, and everyone jumped into their seats.

Without a word he put his coat in the cloakroom and went to his desk. He rang the bell to take up books, and everyone quietly opened their readers.

Everyone took turns reading paragraphs. Rose stared out the window at the trees. Then she spotted Oscar Hensley making faces at George Cooley. George's face flushed bright red from trying not to laugh. Then he could not hold back anymore and laughed loudly.

Professor Crowe sprang to his feet. His

eyebrows arched as he searched the boys' side of the room. Then he spied George's red face. He strode over without a word, grabbed George's arm, and dragged him to the front of the room.

"Let this be an example to you all," Professor Crowe declared.

He whipped George across the shoulders with his cane switch. He struck George six times. Each time every shoulder in the room hunched as if it too had been struck.

Then George sat down, his head bent, sniffing quietly. Rose felt sick. It scared her to see a grown-up hit a child. She had never seen a teacher who was so rough. It made her angry and scared and sad all at the same time.

Finally it was time for recess. On their way to the cloakroom, some of the boys stopped by the stove to warm their hands. They kicked the stove's feet, and it skidded just a bit. The stovepipe was beginning to tilt a little.

On the girls' playground the Fourth Reader girls stood in a knot, their hands tucked under their arms for warmth.

"Teacher hadn't any need to whip George," Rose declared. "He's just plain mean."

"My papa's on the school committee," Blanche said. "He said the committee couldn't find another teacher so soon after Miss Pimberton left. He said we must be good and endure it. But I don't know how I can."

When the bell rang to call the children back to books, Rose found the boys huddled by the front door, whispering and giggling. Just before she reached the door, they all rushed inside.

She followed them up the stairs. As she walked into the classroom, she saw them each pass by the stove and give it another kick. The last one, Jess Robinett, gave it a hard poke. Then he jumped out of the way just as the stovepipe pulled loose from the ceiling. The whole pipe began to lean.

"Look out!" Rose shouted. Then it fell to the floor with a crash and a great clattering. A cloud of black dust exploded from the top end of the pipe. Smoke and sparks rose toward the ceiling.

"What in tarnation?" Professor Crowe growled, rushing into the room. Professor Curty, who taught Fifth and Sixth Readers across the hall, poked his head in.

"Everyone all right?" he asked.

"I believe so," Professor Crowe said

with a dark scowl. "Looks like the pipe worked itself loose. I expect I'll have to cancel lessons till it can be fixed."

Professor Crowe looked at the stove and kicked at the pipe. Then he stooped to look at something on the floor. He put his finger on a spot on the floor where one of the stove feet had sat. The wood was brighter there.

Then Professor Crowe stood up slowly, turned, and looked around the room at all the students. His face flushed red. His eyes narrowed.

"Who called out?" Professor Crowe yelled. "Who saw what happened here?"

All the children looked at one another and shrugged, except Rose. She felt fluttery in her chest and she could hardly breathe. Lula and Blanche and Lydia glanced at her, but she looked at the floor.

Professor Crowe raised his cane switch.

"Who shouted 'Look out'?" he roared.

Rose dared not speak. Her legs tingled with fear and her neck flushed hot. The room was deathly quiet.

Professor Crowe's eyes flashed, and he

slammed the cane switch down on the top of the nearest desk—WHACK! Everyone flinched.

"Very well," he said. "None of you are willing to step forward and name the person who moved the stove so the pipe would fall, so you will all be punished. Every last one of you will do your lessons during recess, for the entire school session! Now you may as well go to your homes. We will take up books again in the morning when the pipe has been repaired."

Rose's stomach churned as she went to the cloakroom.

"Are you going to tell?" Blanche whispered.

"No," Rose said proudly. She knew she could be as brave as the boys who had played the trick. "I wouldn't tell even if he beat me with his old stick."

CHAPTER 7

The Last Straw

The next day the boys and girls tried to be as good as they could. No one made any funny faces, and there were no tricks played. At recess, Professor Crowe made everyone stay inside and continue their lessons. The only time they could relax was when Teacher left the room. Then everyone let out a sigh.

At last Friday came. Rose stayed in at noon to eat at her desk and read from her new book. All the other students went outside to eat or walk home to have their dinner with their families.

Before the end of the hour, Jess Robinett walked into the classroom and looked around.

"Is Teacher back yet?" he whispered to Rose. He was clutching his coat.

"No," Rose said.

Jess opened his coat. Inside it he had a raccoon pelt. He dashed out and climbed back down the stairs. Rose followed him and watched as he took the pelt and dragged it along the floor of the hall and all the way up the stairs. He made sure to swipe each step with the pelt.

Then he dragged the pelt into the classroom, all around the floor, along the walls, and then into the cloakroom.

"What are you doing?" Rose asked. She knew it was some kind of trick, but she couldn't imagine what it could be.

"Just you be quiet about it," he said. "You'll find out soon enough." Then he stuffed the pelt into the sleeve of his coat and hung it up on a peg.

When lessons began, Rose could hardly concentrate. She kept wondering about the trick. Jess kept his head down and sneaked a sidelong look at Rose now and then. He grinned and his face turned crimson with silent laughing.

Finally Professor Crowe said it was time for the Friday spelldown. All the children got up and stood in a line at the front. Professor Crowe sat at his desk, reading out the words and listening to the spellers.

After a little while, Rose heard dogs barking somewhere down the hill in town. It sounded like hunting dogs—raccoon-hunting dogs.

Suddenly Jess raised his hand.

"I'm sure you can wait until the spell-down is over," Professor Crowe said.

"Gee, Teacher," Jess pleaded. "I got to go. Honest."

"Oh well, go on then," Professor Crowe said with a wave of his hand.

As the others continued spelling, Rose watched Jess race into the cloakroom. He took an extra-long time getting his coat. Then he raced out of the cloakroom and down the stairs. Rose noticed that he had left the door slightly open.

Professor Crowe was about to give the next word when there was a loud noise in the stairway. Suddenly the school echoed with the sound of barking and howling dogs. A wave of nervous giggling broke out among the scholars.

Professor Crowe stood up.

"What the dickens is it now?" he

yelled. He strode to the door and reached out to grab the handle when it burst open on its own. A big brown and black hunting dog jumped up, its face grinning and its tongue lolling. Its front paws landed right on Professor Crowe's chest, and he went down with a thud.

Rose and the other girls let out a shriek. Six more dogs poured in through the door, all trampling right over Professor Crowe. He waved his arms and legs wildly in the air, trying to get up.

Now all the children were screaming and laughing. The dogs were howling and barking at one another. They raced around the room, their noses to the floor.

Children flew in every direction trying to get out of the way. Desks tipped over and hit the floor with loud bangs.

Professor Crowe stood up and swore.

His clothes were covered with muddy paw prints. Professor Curty came running from across the hallway.

"What in heaven's name!" he shouted.

Then one of the dogs raised its head and set up a fearful new howling. It darted into the cloakroom. All the other dogs followed, and they all began to snarl at one another again. The dogs were fighting.

Now all the teachers in the school had come to the door, their eyes wide. A cluster of children from the other readers peered behind them.

"I knew I should never have come to this vile place!" Professor Crowe screamed, waving his arms in the air. "Bunch of savages."

Suddenly the dogs burst out of the cloakroom. Two of them were growling deeply and tugging at a long black coat.

With each pull the cloth made a ripping
sound. Then they were all snapping at it,
trying to steal it away from the others.

Professor Crowe's eyes popped. "My
coat!" he shrieked. "The filthy varmints
have got my coat!"

Suddenly one of the dogs snatched the
raccoon pelt out of one of the torn sleeves.
He dashed out the door between the legs

of the teachers and students. Rose could hear the dog bounding back down the stairs. All the other dogs followed, howling and snapping as they went.

Professor Crowe reached down and picked up his tattered coat. He looked around the room. His face blazed bright red.

"A bunch of good-for-nothing heathens!" he exploded, shaking his fist.

Then he whirled to face the teachers standing in the doorway.

"This is the last straw!" he yelled. "The school committee will pay for the damage, and my fare back to Springfield. I won't spend another day in this godforsaken place. Good day and good riddance!"

Then he stomped out, pushing his way through the crowd, dragging the torn coat after him.

CHAPTER 8

A Useful Lesson

Professor Crowe did leave town that very night. Rose did not snitch on Jess Robinett, but everyone knew he was the one who had tricked Professor Crowe. Jess's father punished him, but he was treated like a hero at school.

For a while there was no teacher for the Fourth Reader. Mama said classes might be canceled for the whole session. But then an announcement was made. Miss Pimberton was coming back! Except now she was to be called Mrs.

Honeycutt, because she had married Eldon Honeycutt, an engineer for the railroad.

After that Rose looked forward to every day of school. Mrs. Honeycutt was the best teacher Rose had ever had. She led the class in singing and taught them play-party games. She read wonderful stories to them from books and played crack-the-whip with them at recess. She was gentle and patient and always had a smile. Even the boys obeyed her.

She was very clever, too. One day Rose went to the cloakroom before recess. But she couldn't find the tam-o'-shanter Mama had made her.

Hot tears blurred her eyes as she searched frantically among the other coats. She looked on the floor and along the shelves of dinner pails. But the hat wasn't

65

anywhere to be found. Rose just knew someone had taken it!

"Now, now. Don't fret," Mrs. Honeycutt soothed her. "I'm sure it will turn up. She took her own scarf and put it around Rose's head. "There! Now go and play. We will see what's to be done after recess."

When Rose came back from recess, she noticed that Mrs. Honeycutt had something sitting on her desk. It was a branch shaped like the letter *T*. After everyone had hung up their hats and coats and settled in their desks, Mrs. Honeycutt stood before the class, holding the stick in her hand. Her face was very stern.

Everyone looked at one another in surprise. Mrs. Honeycutt had never whipped anyone, but it looked like she meant to whip someone with that stick.

"I'm very sorry to say that it seems

someone in this room may have taken the hat of another scholar," she said. "It was the blue tam-o'-shanter belonging to Rose Wilder."

Blanche gasped and looked at Rose. Then every eye was on her. Rose stared at her desktop, and her neck burned hot.

"Perhaps this was a mistake," Mrs. Honeycutt said. "But in case it was not, I have collected this stick in the woods." She held up the stick to show the class. "It is a known fact that a hickory branch in the shape of a T can find a thief. If I throw it in the air, it will land on the top of the head of the person who took the hat.

"If someone did take the hat, or knows of its whereabouts, he or she should speak now, and all will be forgiven."

A nervous titter ran through the room as everyone twisted and turned in their

67

seats, looking for the thief to stand up and confess. But no one did.

"Very well, then," Mrs. Honeycutt said. "We will let the stick tell us. " She waved the stick and drew her arm back to throw it.

Suddenly Lula Faddis shouted out, "Almeda done it! She dodged when you went to throw the stick, Teacher. I seen her."

"Yes, I saw," Mrs. Honeycutt said.

She walked down the rows of desks to where Almeda Fike was sitting. Almeda's face was crimson.

Almeda was one of the poor country girls who came to school with no hat or scarf to keep her head warm in the bitter cold. Rose's heart ached to see her slumped in her seat, trembling like a trapped animal.

 68

Mrs. Honeycutt put her hand on Almeda's shoulder.

"Almeda, do you know where Rose's hat is?" she asked gently.

Almeda stared at her desk and silently nodded. A tear fell from her cheek.

"Where is it, dear?"

Almeda mumbled some words that

Rose couldn't hear.

"Children, I will return presently," Mrs. Honeycutt said. "Please remain in your seats and study your lessons."

Mrs. Honeycutt and Almeda put on their coats and walked out of the room and down the stairs.

As soon as they heard the front door of the school close, everyone jumped up from their desks and ran to the windows.

They saw Mrs. Honeycutt walking with Almeda through the snow to the edge of the playground. Almeda kicked away some snow near an old log. She reached down and picked up the tam-o'-shanter. Rose breathed a sigh of relief.

Mrs. Honeycutt took the hat and brushed off the snow. Then she squatted down and took off her own scarf. She tied it around Almeda's head, tucking the ends into her threadbare coat. Her breath came in puffs of steam. She was speaking to Almeda.

Almeda wiped her eyes. Then Mrs. Honeycutt hugged Almeda, patted her on the shoulder, and sent her to the horse shed.

Mrs. Honeycutt watched Almeda untether her mule, climb up on it, and ride off. Then she turned back toward the schoolhouse.

The children scrambled back in their seats. Everyone wondered what would become of Almeda.

Mrs. Honeycutt came back, took off her coat in the cloakroom, and stood by the heater stove.

"Rose's hat is back where it belongs," she said. "And I have sent Almeda home for the day. She knows she made a mistake, and she is very sorry for it. Everyone makes a mistake from time to time. We must remember that they who forgive most will be most forgiven.

"When Almeda returns to school, no one will tease her or I promise they will be punished. Now let us begin our lessons."

Rose looked at Mrs. Honeycutt with a brimming heart. She knew that no one could ever be more kind or fair.

After Mrs. Honeycutt rang the bell to end that day's lessons, Rose waited to talk with her.

"Thank you ever so much, Mrs. Honeycutt," Rose said.

"You are most welcome, Rose," Teacher answered.

Rose stood there, thinking and looking at the hickory branch lying on the corner of the desk.

"Is it really true, about the stick knowing who is a thief?" Rose asked.

"What do you think?" Mrs. Honeycutt asked, a twinkle in her eye.

Rose thought a moment. "I think only a thief would think it is true."

Mrs. Honeycutt beamed. "Then you have learned a useful lesson, Rose," she said.

Rose thought about school as she walked home that day. She felt so lucky to have a wonderful new teacher who taught her useful things, as well as her own best friend. She looked forward to school every day. So much had changed since Rose's dreaded first day of school in Missouri when she felt alone and out of place. Now she knew she belonged.

THE COMPLETE
LAURA CHAPTER BOOK COLLECTION

Adapted from the Little House books
by Laura Ingalls Wilder
Illustrated by Renée Graef and Doris Ettlinger